Ned's Forgetful Nana

Om KIDZ
An imprint of Om Books International

Om Kidz | Om Books International

Reprinted in 2023

Corporate & Editorial Office
A-12, Sector 64, Noida 201 301
Uttar Pradesh, India
Phone: +91 120 477 4100
Email: editorial@ombooks.com
Website: www.ombooksinternational.com

ISBN: 978-93-52760-30-5

Printed in India

10 9 8 7 6 5 4 3 2

Sales Office
107, Ansari Road, Darya Ganj
New Delhi 110 002, India
Phone: +91 11 4000 9000
Email: sales@ombooks.com
Website: www.ombooks.com

Ned's Forgetful Nana

Paste your photograph here

My name is

In a **nearby** town, lives a **nice** boy. His **name** is **Ned.**

Ned is **new** to the **neighbourhood** but people easily **notice** him because he is just so **nice.**

His grandmother
is a **neat** woman.

She is **never** mean to **Ned.**

Ned calls her **'Nana'.**

Nana keeps asking **Ned** to cut his **nails.** But **Ned** always forgets.

One day, **Ned** falls sick.

Nana asks him to take a **nap.**
She looks after **Ned** like a **nurse.**

She wants to make him
a **noodle** soup.

She has seen a **new** recipe in the **newspaper.**

But she does **not** remember where she kept her glasses. She looks under the **napkin** in the kitchen.

Next, she looks in **Ned's** room. But she cannot find them.

Nana tries to leave **Ned's** room without making a **noise.**

But **Ned** wakes up. “What are you looking for, **Nana?”** he asks.

"My glasses, dear. I cannot find them," she says.

Ned begins to laugh.
They were sitting on her
nose the whole time!

"**Nana!** Your glasses are right there, on your **nose!**" says **Ned.**

Nana chuckles and pushes the glasses higher on her **nose.**

Later, **Nana** makes a soup like **never** before.

Ned drinks it all up.

He feels much better **now.**

Nana tucks **Ned** in bed.

“**Never** forget to cut your **nails** again. That is how you fall sick,” she says to **Ned.**

Ned puts his arms around **Nana.**

He gives her a tight hug.

Nana knows best!

Know your words

Naming words

name
nurse
Ned
noodle
neighbourhood
newspaper
Nana
napkin
nails
nose
nap

Describing words

nearby
new
nice
neat

Doing words

notice

Sight words

noise
never
not

Help Nana find her glasses.

Find the below words in the word search.

F	G	V	H	R	X	P	E
I	J	R	A	N	E	A	T
E	N	O	O	D	L	E	R
N	I	O	O	D	L	W	C
I	P	U	O	N	N	N	A
C	N	N	E	V	E	R	I
E	M	F	U	H	W	A	L
R	H	Q	T	X	W	P	T

NICE

NEW

NEVER

NEAT

NOODLE

Based on the story, match the following.

Nice •   • 

Neat •   • 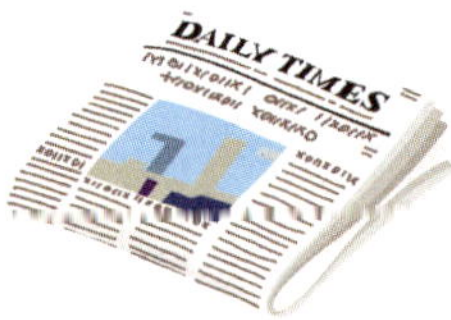

Recipe •   • 

Soup •   •